EVANSTON PUBLIC LIBRARY

P9-BZS-689

JPicture Tsuba.M

Tsubakiyama, Margaret.

Mei-Mei loves the
   morning /
      c1999.

JUN 07 1999

MEI-MEI
LOVES THE MORNING

WRITTEN BY Margaret Holloway Tsubakiyama
PAINTINGS BY Cornelius Van Wright & Ying-Hwa Hu

~ Albert Whitman & Company ~
Morton Grove, Illinois

EVANSTON PUBLIC LIBRARY
CHILDREN'S DEPARTMENT
1703 ORRINGTON AVENUE
EVANSTON, ILLINOIS 60201

Library of Congress Cataloging-in-Publication Data
Tsubakiyama, Margaret Holloway.
Mei-Mei loves the morning / by Margaret Holloway Tsubakiyama ;
illustrated by Cornelius Van Wright and Ying-Hwa Hu.
p. cm.
Summary:
A young Chinese girl and her grandfather enjoy a typical morning riding on
Grandpa's bicycle to meet friends in the park.
ISBN 0-8075-5039-6
[1. Grandfathers—Fiction. 2. China—Fiction.]
I. Van Wright, Cornelius, ill. II. Hu, Ying-Hwa, ill. III. Title.
PZ7.T789Me 1999
[E]—dc21 97-26675
CIP AC

Text © copyright 1999 by Margaret Holloway Tsubakiyama.
Illustrations © copyright 1999 by Cornelius Van Wright and Ying-Hwa Hu.
Published in 1999 by Albert Whitman & Company,
6340 Oakton Street, Morton Grove, Illinois 60053.
Published simultaneously in Canada by General Publishing,
Limited, Toronto. All rights reserved. No part of this book may be
reproduced or transmitted in any form or by any means, electronic
or mechanical, including photocopying, recording, or by any
information storage and retrieval system, without permission in
writing from the publisher.
Printed in the United States of America.
10 9 8 7 6 5 4 3 2 1

The illustrations are rendered in
watercolor and pencil on illustration board.
The text typeface is Maiandra.
The design is by Scott Piehl.

To my husband,
for taking me to China.
— M. H. T.

To En-szu and En-wei.
— C. V. W. and Y. H.

MEI-MEI loves the morning. When she wakes up, she always hears Bai-Ling rustling impatiently in his cage and Grandpa's slippers slip-slapping on the kitchen floor. Mother and Father are still asleep, but Mei-Mei jumps out of bed.

Mei-Mei loves the morning because Grandpa lets her
unzip the night cover on Bai-Ling's cage. Mei-Mei looks
inside the cage. Bai-Ling's eyes are shining in the darkness.
When Mei-Mei lifts off the cover, Bai-Ling begins to sing.

Mei-Mei fills a tiny bowl with millet and another with water for Bai-Ling's breakfast. Grandpa fills bowls with rice porridge for Mei-Mei and himself. Mei-Mei puts pickled vegetables on hers. They are so sour that her mouth puckers when she eats them.

After breakfast they put on their coats and go down to the lobby where Grandpa keeps his bicycle. Grandpa gives Bai-Ling's cage to Mei-Mei. It is so heavy that she needs both hands to hang it on the handlebars.

Slowly, slowly, they ride down the block. Mei-Mei sits at the front of the bicycle. A cool wind blows, but it's warm in Grandpa's arms.

Even though it is still early, the street is busy. The peddlers are setting up their stalls, waiting for the first customers of the day. Everyone is in a hurry. Only the farmers are still asleep, snoring in their trucks full of potatoes and cabbage. "Wake up, sleepyheads!" calls a man as he rides by. "It's morning!"

At the corner Grandpa stops to talk with the cobbler. Mei-Mei watches the cobbler tap on a lady's red shoe with his tiny hammer. He polishes the shoe with a soft cloth until it shines like a lacquer bowl.

Grandpa lifts Mei-Mei off the bicycle. The cobbler lets her try the shoes on. Grandpa smiles when Mei-Mei walks like a princess in the beautiful red shoes.

Down the street they ride, through the round moon gate, and into the park. Grandpa hugs Mei-Mei to make sure she doesn't fall as they go over the bump.

In the park their friends are waiting at their favorite bench
beneath the plum tree. They have saved a place for Mei-Mei
and Grandpa on the bench and one for Bai-Ling in the tree.

Grandpa lifts Mei-Mei up to hang Bai-Ling's cage on a branch. The whole tree is filled with songbirds, and the whole tree is singing.

They stay at the park all morning long. Mei-Mei and her friend Xiao-Chen do tai-chi with Grandpa. They pretend to tame a tiger and to grab a bird by the feathers of its tail. They pretend they are carrying big balls in their hands. Everyone moves slowly and carefully. Then they stop, still as white cranes in the grass.

After they exercise Grandpa gives Mei-Mei a jar of tea.
The warm jar feels good in her hands. Grandpa and his friends
swirl their tea and drink and talk. Mei-Mei and Xiao-Chen just
swirl theirs and watch the tea leaves all fall down.

The sun is already hot when they leave the park. Grandpa puts his cap on Mei-Mei's head. His cap is so big that from under its brim Mei-Mei can barely see all the bicycles. Some carry vegetables to market; others bring students to school. One bicycle is even piled high with mattresses.

Mei-Mei sees a pig poking its head from a basket. The pig squeals angrily as the bicycle rides by. Mei-Mei snuggles deeper into Grandpa's arms.

They stop at the corner. The lao-bing man's stove is hot, and his pancakes sizzle.

"How many today?" he asks. Mei-Mei holds up four fingers. The lao-bing man wraps four crisp pancakes in a sheet of newspaper and hands them to her. Mei-Mei holds them in her pocket, warm all the way home.

Grandpa parks his bicycle in the lobby. Mei-Mei jumps off the bicycle into his arms.

"I love the morning, Grandpa," says Mei-Mei.

己
巷

Grandpa hugs her tight. "I love it, too," he says.